To:

From:

CAN YOU PUT ME TO BED?

THE TALE OF THE NOT-SO-SLEEPY SLOTH

WORDS BY ERIN GUENDELSBERGER
PICTURES BY ANDOTWIN

sourcebooks
wonderland

I am having such a great day.

I never want it to end!

The sun is already going down, and

can you believe it? I'm not even sleepy.

What do you mean, it's bedtime?

I just told you I'm not tired.

I'll brush my teeth and take a bath if I have to,
but I don't want to go to bed yet.

Can you dry my hair for me?

It's always better when someone else does it.

These hairdos are SO great.

I can't go to bed now!

I'll ruin my favorite one!

OK, OK. I put on my pajamas.

Uh-oh! I don't think I got the pants right. Would you tap on the pajama pants that match my top?

Now I'm ready for…

…a sloth dance party*! Woo-hoo! Dance with me!

I'm not sleepy in my pajamas.

*It's a sloth, so it's a slo-mo dance party.

FINE. I'll get into bed, but we forgot something very important—my stuffed animals! I have to say good night to each one.

May I please have my bear? And heart?

And hedgehog? And bunny? And baby sloth?

Just tip the book to drop them on the bed.

Oof! Good night, Bear!

Sweet dreams, Heart!

See you in the morning, Hedgie!

Night-night, Bunny!

Sleep tight, Baby Sloth!

I think there are too many animals now.

I'll keep just one. Will you shake the rest off the bed?

That's better, though I promise I won't fall asleep.

You can even turn off the light.

That won't bother me.

Clap once to turn it off.

Ack! It's too dark!

Clap twice to turn on my night-light.

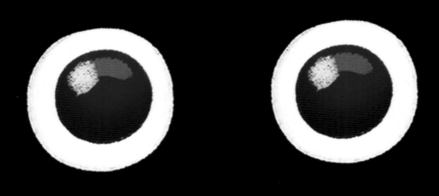

Thank you. That's just right.

You know what else would help? A song.

Can you sing me your favorite lullaby?

I'm not sleepy...

even when someone sings to me.

WAIT! I am so thirsty!
I need a drink of water right away!

That's better, but I can't fall asleep yet. Could you maybe rub my back for a little while?

Mmm. If you want to give me a kiss, you can.

That won't make me tired.

If you whisper I love you, guess what?

I'll say, I love you too.

I'm still…

not…

sleepy…

SWEET DREAMS

For my sister Sarah, and all those years of whispering through bedtime.
—EG

For all the little sleepy sloths out there, you know who you are, go to bed!
—AT

Copyright © 2021 by Sourcebooks
Text by Erin Guendelsberger
Illustrations by AndoTwin
Cover and internal design © 2021 by Allison Sundstrom/Sourcebooks

Sourcebooks and the colophon are registered trademarks of Sourcebooks.

All book illustrations have been sketched and colored in Photoshop with a Wacom Intuos tablet.

Published by Sourcebooks Wonderland, an imprint of Sourcebooks Kids
P.O. Box 4410, Naperville, Illinois 60567–4410
(630) 961-3900
sourcebookskids.com

Library of Congress Cataloging-in-Publication Data is on file with the publisher.

Source of Production: PrintPlus Limited, Shenzhen, Guangdong Province, China
Date of Production: May 2021
Run Number: 5021597

Printed and bound in China.
PP 10 9 8 7 6 5 4 3 2 1